This book is dedicated to Ms. Jesika Boykins; the awesome 2nd grade teacher that she is!

This book is also dedicated to my family, the best family ever! A special thank you to my Mommy for all her help in making this book possible.

Dear Ms. Boykins,

 I hope you're having a nice summer. I wanted to tell you that it rained here last night and today I saw a dolphin in a puddle. It was very shy.

Your student,
Helena

P.S. What should I do now?

Dear Helena,
　　　My summer is going well, thank you.
I'm sorry to tell you, but there is no dolphin in your
puddle. They are as big as a car or a bicycle. How
could it fit? And dolphins aren't very shy. They're
quite social.

Your teacher,
Ms. Boykins

Dear Ms. Boykins,

       Today I fed the dolphin a pineapple. He's not shy anymore. And when I was playing with him, I found out he has a purple belly!

Your student,
Helena

Dear Helena,
       Dolphins eat fish, not pineapple.
They can have a pink or light gray belly, but
not a purple belly.

Your teacher,
Ms. Boykins

Dear Ms. Boykins,

     My dolphin is not coming out of the puddle and the puddle is drying up, so I got him a bucket of water. By the way, I need more information on what to do now. Thanks.

Your student,
Helena

Dear Helena,
    It's impossible for you to have a dolphin in your bucket. Because they are too big to fit in one and they only live in the ocean or in the Amazon River. The Amazon is where the dolphins with the pink bellies live.

Your teacher,
Ms. Boykins

P.S. Dolphins are mammals.

Dear Ms. Boykins,

Thank you for the information. Today I held another pineapple out for the dolphin. He came out and ate it! I think I will name him Billy. I also held out a fish like you suggested. He didn't like that too much!

Your students,
Helena and Billy

P.S. Billy loves your notes. He thinks they're kind of funny. He also loves being patted.

Dear Helena,

I'm sorry to say this, but once again, it's impossible to have a pineapple-eating, purple-bellied dolphin in a bucket. I know you think it's not. But it really is. I do hope you're having a nice summer. Thanks for writing.

Your teacher,
Ms. Boykins

P.S. Dolphins already have their own name because they have their own call. It's like their name in dolphin language.

Dear Ms. Boykins,

　　Billy accidentally knocked his bucket over like a silly dolphin. But it rained last night, so don't worry he's got water.

Your students,
Helena and Billy

Dear Helena,
   Dolphins are actually very smart. They are some of the smartest creatures on earth. They might even be smarter than humans. He will be okay.

Your teacher,
Ms. Boykins

Dear Ms. Boykins,

Today I read Billy your notes again. He laughed and smiled. He's so sweet! He got hungry so I fed him some more pineapple.

Your students,
Helena and Billy

Dear Helena,
　　Today I went to the beach and actually saw a dolphin. I thought of you. And, for the last time, dolphins eat fish.

Your teacher,

Ms. Boykins

Dear Ms. Boykins,

  Today I went to the beach too. I took Billy with me. He is playing with another dolphin right now. He's really having a lot of fun.

Your students,
Helena and Billy

P.S. I let Billy go. Don't feel bad for us. We had many good times together!

Dear Helena,

There's a dolphin in my pool!

Your confused teacher,
Ms. Boykins

Made in the USA
Lexington, KY
06 November 2015